Just Like You

by Robert Kroupa

illustrations by Hannah E. Harrison

SEVEN LEGS PRESS

In a little tin cottage
in the deep Piney Forest,
lived a field mouse named Henry
and his spider friend, Boris.

Boris had seven legs
that were really quite strong,
but his last leg was curled,
so he pulled it along.

As he crept and crawled
over shady pathways,
Henry waited for Boris
so they could both play.

Though Henry was fast,
and ran all the mouse races,
those he passed on the track
made nasty mouse faces.

And since Henry was deaf,
his ears folded in half,
he couldn't hear other mice
tease him or laugh.

SPIDER BEARD SET SAIL ON THE SAL

So Boris spun webs with words Henry could read and wove stories in them for Henry to see.

Other spiders were bullies,
acting mean, poking fun.
"Your webs aren't like ours,
and you can't even run!"

"I *can* spin webs like yours,"
Boris held up his head,
"but I have other ways,
mine are like this instead."

Still they were mean,
saying Boris was lame,
and that Henry was dumb,
"You're just not the same!"

"We are different," said Boris.
Henry signed, "That is true."
"But in so many ways,
we are *just like you*."

Henry picked Boris up
and they slowly went home,
to their little tin house,
where they lived all alone.

They stayed by themselves
near the narrow cold creek,
under roofs of green leaves,
they played hide and go seek.

Henry swam in the river
and climbed up the trees.
Boris read in the sun
with a book on his knees.

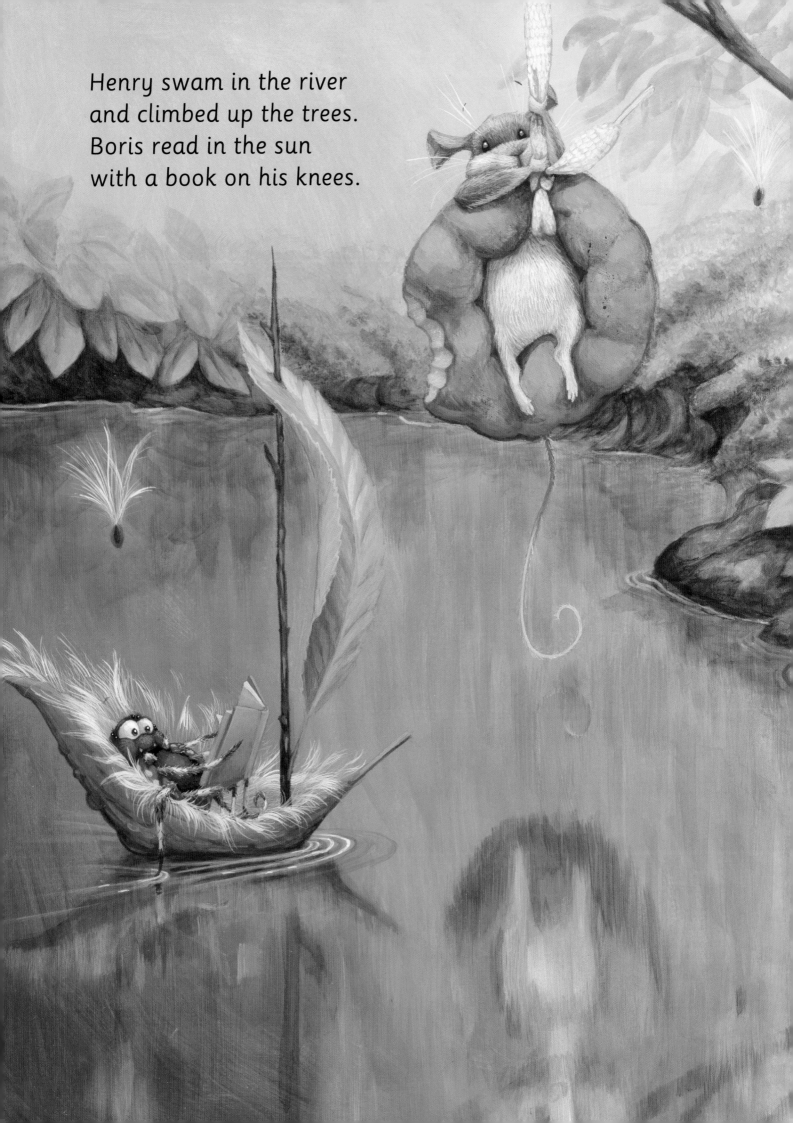

But then one hot day
while Boris lay sleeping,
Henry saw an orange spark,
then saw a flame leaping.

Henry signed with his paws,
"Wake up! There's a fire!"
They saw flames spread wider,
then watched them grow higher.

The wind began blowing,
fire danced all around.
Soon their green forest
would burn to the ground!

"We must tell the others!"
Boris started to weave,
quickly spinning a web
for them all to see.

Henry tied a gold bell
to the end of his tail.
Then they raced up the hill
with their flag like a sail.

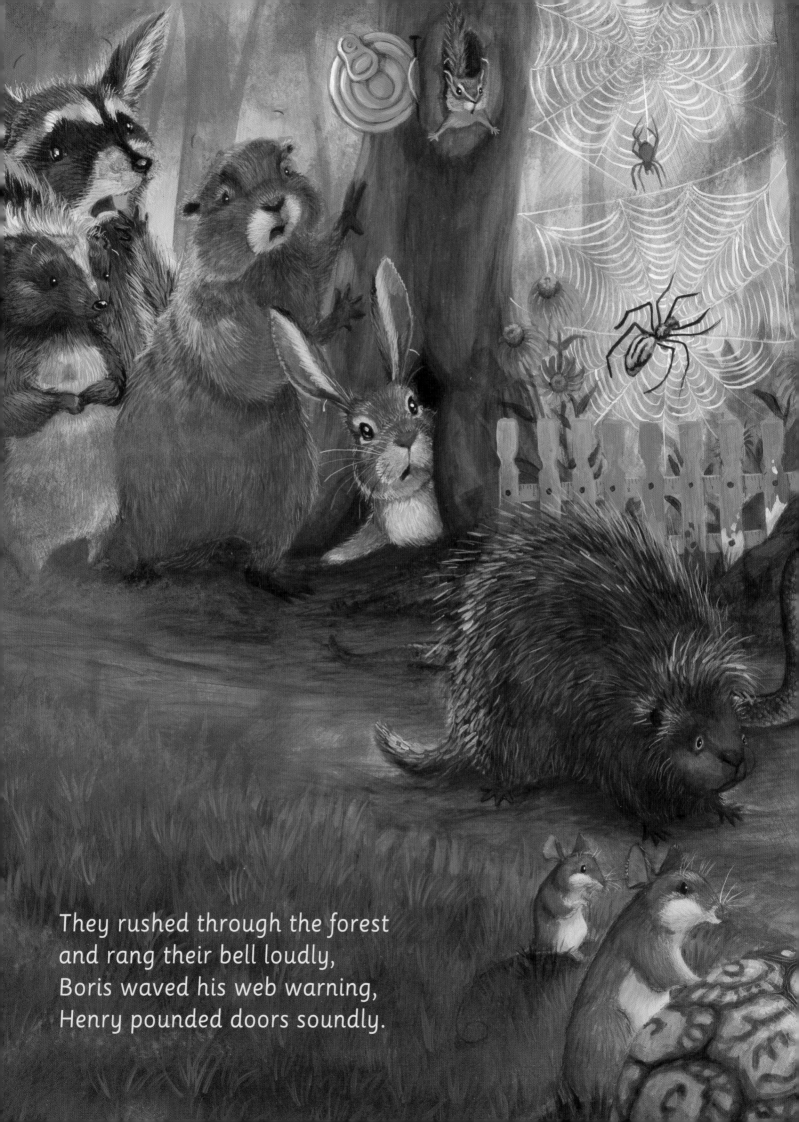

They rushed through the forest
and rang their bell loudly,
Boris waved his web warning,
Henry pounded doors soundly.

The others poured out
from their burrows and lairs.
To smell the gray smoke
and see soot in the air.

All cried when they saw
the flames in the forest,
then they ran from the fire
led by Henry and Boris.

When it started to rain
everyone stopped to stare.
Flames sputtered and hissed,
making steam in the air.

They all gathered 'round
as drops fell from the sky.
When the smoke fizzled out...

...“We are saved!” rose the cry.

They looked to each other,
and each of them knew,
it was wrong to be mean
to such friends as these two.

They hoisted up Henry
and then lifted Boris,
their many small voices
ringing out like a chorus.

"Because now we all see
that it really *is* true.
You *are* just like us,
and we are

Just
Like
You!"

Edited by Sarah Stonich

Designed by Zachary Marell

Chicago, IL

Website address: www.justlikeyoufoundation.org

Library of Congress Cataloging-in-Publication Data

Kroupa, Robert J.
  Just like you / by Robert J. Kroupa.
    p.   cm.
  Summary: Henry, a deaf field mouse, and his friend Boris, a spider with one
lame leg, are teased by the other animals until a disaster realizes they are not
so different, after all.
  ISBN 978-0-9825503-4-2
  [1. Stories in rhyme. 2. Disabilities--Fiction. 3. Deaf--Fiction. 4. Friendship--
Fiction. 5. Mice--Fiction. 6. Spiders--Fiction.] I. Title.
  PZ8.3.K8999Jus 2011
  [E]--dc22
                                   2009049790
Manufactured in the United States of America
10 9 8 7 6 5 4 3 2